Grandma's Silent Auction
July
BY: Michael James

Copyright © 2020 by Michael James

All rights reserved.

No part of this book may be reproduced in any form or by any electronic or mechanical means, including information storage and retrieval systems, without written permission from the author, except for the use of brief quotations in a book review.

CHAPTER ONE
CIARA

For the past three days, I've been staying with Grams at her mansion. She didn't feel comfortable with me staying at my apartment with an unknown psycho out there after me. I haven't even been able to leave the house without her driver taking me. She is thrilled to death that Mr. July has bodyguards around him all the time. I tried to get it out of her who he is, but she left that a mystery. So, I still only have a name - Jasper Collins. I am off to meet him right now.

I make myself comfortable in the plane's seat and put on my seatbelt. I stare out the window, watching another plane taxiing down the runway. I am not sure if it's coming or going. I turn my head when the stewardess asks if I'd like a drink. Yes, I would love one, but I'm not allowed to have anything worth drinking,

I want to say. The rules of the new guy, no alcohol. Heaven forbid I have a drink to calm my nerves. So far this new guy is getting on my nerves and I haven't even met him yet.

"I'll take a bottle of water, please."

She hands me the water and moves on. I go back to watching out the window. I wish this plane would get in the air already. I am tempted to run. I still hate the take-off part. It makes me antsy and gives me a slight panic attack. It isn't helping with the added stress of wondering who is out to ruin me. Once I'm in the air, I'm fine and the landing is a huge relief. I hope that stands true today. As much as this new guy is giving out orders before we even meet, I am looking forward to getting away from home. I am hoping in the month I'm gone the police can figure out who the hell destroyed my shop.

I move my elbow off the armrest when the person next to me bumps it. I didn't even look to see who it was. I put my head back on the headrest, close my eyes, and take a deep breath. I was hoping by being in first class, nobody would be seated next to me.

"Nervous?"

I open my eyes and turn to look at the person who's voice caught my attention. Damn, he's sexy as hell. My voice squeaks. *"A little bit."* Why isn't he on

Gram's list of men? I mean really, he's super-hot. He screams sex. *"I don't really like flying."*

"What is it about flying you don't like?"

"The take-off."

"Want a drink? It might calm your nerves."

"I'm not allowed."

"Hmm, that's interesting."

"Trust me, I would love one, but it's against the rules."

"Well, I guess it's a good thing you have me next to you. I'll distract you and you'll never know we left land."

I laugh. If he only knew it's already working. I'm totally distracted. I can't help the feeling of wanting to touch him, run my fingers through his dirty blond hair. To put my lips to his perfectly colored ones. I wish his shirt was off. I mean, unbuttoned a little more so that I could see his smooth, tanned chest more. Man, I need a drink. A tall glass of him would work, too! Good God, I need sex! Yes, sex would totally distract me right now.

"Where are you off to?"

"Tennessee."

"I know that I'm on the same flight. I meant, why are you going to Tennessee?"

"I am going to meet a month-long blind date that my Grandma set up."

"You don't sound thrilled about that."

"I'm not if I'm being honest."

"Why not?"

"Just because. Honestly, it's a long story, but to shorten it, my Grandma put me in a silent auction and all these men bought me."

"How many men?"

"Ten."

"Hmm, how much did you go for?"

"I don't know. She wouldn't tell me. Guy number one said he paid over a hundred grand, though."

"Did he get his money's worth?"

"If you are asking if I put out, that is none of your business."

"C'mon, this is an interesting story."

"No, I didn't sleep with him." He doesn't need to know that's a lie.

He smiles and winks at me. I look away, embarrassed that I told him all that. His hand takes mine in his. He turns my hand so that my palm is turned up. He lightly brushes his fingertips over my palm. I close my eyes. Damn this man is turning me on. He sets my hand down on my lap. I wiggle in my seat and cross my legs. He reaches over, touching my lower leg. I am thankful I took the time to shave today.

"You shouldn't sit with your legs crossed during take-off."

"Oh," is all I can manage to say as his fingers trail up my leg toward my knee.

I uncross my legs. I gasp when his hand travels higher up to my thigh. Any higher his hand would be under my skirt, which I'm sure he wouldn't mind doing by the forwardness he's shown. I watch his fingers draw a circle on my skin. He tilts his head to look at me. His very blue eyes feel as if they pierce right through me. His hand slides up a little higher as he comes close to my face.

"Relax, we are practically alone in first class."

I gasp again when he grabs my inner thigh. I swallow hard when his finger brushes my clit through my panties. God help me! I spread my legs a little wider apart. My skirt slides higher up my thighs. I close my eyes when his fingers move my panties off to the side. I bit my lip when he entered two fingers inside me. I grip the armrests as he moves his fingers in and out of me. Fuck, it feels good. When his palm hits against my clit as his fingers fuck me, I try not to moan.

"How was that for distracting you?"

"Huh?"

"We are in the air."

"Oh!"

His hand slips away and he sits upright in his own seat. I squeeze my legs together. I look at him real quick and he winks at me. Sexy-ass fucker and he knows it. I really don't care about that because he can touch me like that again if he wants.

He leans back over into my space. *"I like the way you smell."*

"I don't have perfume on."

He smirks. He puts his fingers close to his nose. *"I know."*

I cross my legs and he laughs. I feel my cheeks blushing. Is it hot on this plane - hotter than normal? Like how high do they have the heat set at in first class?

"I don't..." I'm so flustered. *"I have..."* I take a deep breath. *"I have never let someone I don't know do that to me."*

"I'm hard as fuck right now. If we were alone, I'd fuck you until the sun came up."

I need ice. Like a whole bathtub full of it. A cold shower would work, as well. He's the whole sex factor bundled in a suit. Where did this man come from? I have had men talk to me the way he just did, but there is something different from the tone of his voice. I can tell he's a dominant man. I wonder if he's more dominating than Kaiden is. I desperately need a drink! How am I going to meet Grandma's next guy with a straight face once I land after what he just did to me?

I watch as he gets up from his seat and moves to a different one a few aisles back. He starts talking to the guy in the seat next to him. Was he even supposed to sit next to me? Ugh!

I get out of my seat to head to the restroom. I need to splash some water on my face or something. Just as I am about to pass him, he stops me.

"Where are you going, pretty lady?"

He reaches over discretely and his knuckles run up the back of my leg.

"Not that it's any of your business, but I'm going to the restroom."

"If the bathroom wasn't so small, I'd join you."

"I don't need you to hold my hand, thanks."

"I wasn't thinking about your hand."

"You're an ass!"

Seriously, what in the ever loving hell is wrong with me? I need to get away from this guy. He's a cocky asshole. I wish I stomped on his ego and didn't allow him to touch me. Where the hell is my head at? Thank God, I won't see him again after this damn plane lands.

CHAPTER TWO
CIARA

I waited until everyone else got off the plane in first class before I did. I didn't want to come in contact again with whoever that cocky asshole was. It was bad enough I had to walk past him when returning from the restroom.

Grams told me that there would be security waiting for me as soon as I got off, but I didn't see anyone, so I started looking for my luggage. I highly doubt whoever destroyed my shop followed me to Tennessee. I'm probably safer out of New York right now than I would be if I stayed home.

"Ms. Verbank, I'll get your bags."

"And you are?"

"Sorry, I am Victoria Craig. I work for Jasper Collins." She extends her hand for a handshake.

"Where is the security that was supposed to be waiting for me?"

"I am one of his team members."

"I am just supposed to believe you? What if..." She cuts me off before I can finish my question.

"You can trust me. I am one of his people that looks out for potential dangers. My job is to watch his back from a distance."

"So, he is here?"

"Yes, he's already been taken to the car. He's waiting on you there."

"I only have a small suitcase. I can get it myself."

She snickers, but allows me to get my own luggage. I didn't bring much with me since Grams kept her watchful eye on me. Mr. Collins will have to take me shopping. Yay, I can't wait!

"What do you mean already taken to the car?"

"He just got off a plane."

When we exit the airport, I see a whole security team by a big, black SUV. Who is this guy? How many people does it take to protect one person? I mean seriously, six big, muscular men for one guy?

The closer we get, his bodyguard moves to the side, making way for me to get into the SUV. That is when I see him, the cocky asshole from the plane. My blood is instantly boiling.

"Just goddamn wonderful," I say.

CHAPTER 2

He whips off his sunglasses. *"It's nice to see you again, Ciara."*

"Wish I could say the same."

"What, you don't like my way of distracting your mind from takeoff?" He laughs.

"How about I don't like you, period."

"That's not what my fingers tell me." Is he for real? He actually just smelled his fingers again? *"I think you like me very much."*

"You are an asshole. Has anyone ever told you that? Wait, don't answer. I am sure you've been told many, many times."

He laughs again. *"You are going to be a lot of fun, buttercup. Here I thought I was the entertainer."*

His bodyguard opens the back door to his SUV, then takes my suitcase from me. Jasper uses his hand to tell me to get in first. I really don't want to go with him. I narrow my eyes at him and he smirks. Ugh, he's such a jerk standing there with a smirk the size of Mount Everest on his face. Maybe even bigger. This is going to be one hell of a long month.

I get in the car and he gets in beside me. *"Well, it's about goddamn time!"*

I look at the lady in the seat across from me. Who the hell is she? My thoughts get interrupted when the two of them start chatting it up.

"Ms. Verbank was getting some much needed fresh air."

"Next time don't do it outside the airport where you draw so much attention to yourself. Good thing I had the full security here. Did you even notice the crowd you two had gathered around you?"

"Cynthia, that is why you are my number one. You know when I will need the big boys. I wouldn't have needed them if Ciara didn't draw all the attention."

My neck snaps when I jerk my head to look at him. *"Excuse me? How is that my fault?"*

"Beauty turns heads, buttercup, and people can't help but look at beautiful things."

"Stop calling me buttercup."

"What should I call you? Sweetheart, babe, or honey?"

"Call me Ciara. That is my given name after."

"But nicknames are more endearing."

Cynthia laughs. *"You two are bickering like an old married couple. How cute. Okay, it really isn't cute, it's annoying."*

"Who the hell are you?"

Just like Victoria, she extended her hand. *"Cynthia Cordell. I'm Jasper's manager."*

"Still haven't figured out how to manage him yet, huh? Clearly he acts like a child."

CHAPTER 2

"I might like you, after all, Ms. Verbank."

Jasper leans back in the seat, sprawling his legs out, getting comfortable. He smirks again when I look at him. I roll my eyes. He literally thinks he's all that and then some. How can such an attractive man as himself be such an ass?

"Don't forget, we have a show tonight at eight."

He taps a finger on his temple. *"Got it right here. Did you get Angela to come to my house?"*

"I did, she'll be there by four."

"What is it you do, Jasper?"

"You'll see tonight."

Cynthia glares at me. *"Are you serious or are you joking? You really have no idea who you are sitting next to?"*

"Umm, nope, not joking."

Jasper's phone rung and he retrieved it from his pocket to answer it. Cynthia stares at him as if waiting to find out who called him. I hear him say, *"I see. You will be with her at all times when I am not around."* There's a pause. *"Thanks, Victoria."* He hangs up.

"What did she say?" Cynthia asks.

His eyes travel to me. *"Victoria saw someone at the airport watching you. You are not to go anywhere without me or her accompanying you."*

"I didn't feel like I was being watched. How does she know for sure I have a stalker?"

"We purposely didn't meet you at the gate to see if anyone followed you. I had a guy behind you two walking out of the airport, someone followed you two outside."

"I thought by leaving New York, I'd be safe."

"And you will be if you follow my rules and don't ditch my security team. They know how to protect you."

"Who are you?"

"You'll see tonight."

I lean back in the seat. I cannot believe this is happening. Who the hell is stalking me? I can't think of one person who would be doing this to me. It makes me feel violated and scared.

After a two hour drive from the airport, we dropped Cynthia off in downtown Nashville, after that we arrived at Jasper's home. It's absolutely beautiful. I've never been on a ranch before. I'm looking forward to seeing what goes on at a ranch.

"Your place is beautiful. How long have you lived here?"

"My entire life. This ranch belonged to my grandparents, then my folks, and now me."

"Wow, that's incredible that it has been in your family for so long. Is your family still living here?"

"My grandparents are deceased, so is my father. My mother wanted to move off the ranch and put it on the market when my father passed, so I bought it from her."

"Where does she live now?"

"In a cozy, little home a few miles from here."

"Why only move a few miles away?"

"Maybe once we know each other better we can unload family baggage."

"Fair enough."

"Ready to go inside?"

"Yep!"

Jasper's home is stunning. I love the modern-country feel. Somehow, I feel relaxed here and I've only been here for less than fifteen minutes. Jasper gave me a tour of his four-bedroom home. He left my room as the last one to show me. It's just as gorgeous as the master bedroom. I have plenty of closet space and my own bathroom. I am extremely happy I am not sharing a bed with him. Although his attitude has changed from the plane to arriving here, he's still a cocky asshole.

CHAPTER THREE
JASPER

I just left Ciara with Angela to pick out some new clothing. I had every intention of taking her shopping in downtown Nashville, but I preferred for her to have some privacy. After Millie contacted me and told me about the situation with Ciara's shop, I felt it was best to do shopping at my ranch. I am glad I went that route after learning someone was watching her at the airport. I know she'll be safe with me this month with my bodyguards around us. That gives me some comfort and peace of mind. My team is ready to help find her stalker. I'm giving them a month to do so. I don't know Ciara all that well, but after that plane ride, I know she is too trusting. Don't get me wrong, I highly enjoyed myself. I admit what I did was a dick move, but after touching her leg, I couldn't help myself. Ciara is damn beautiful. You could feel the fear radiating off her. Honestly, it was a good thing we were in public. I don't know if I could have stopped if we weren't. My jeans were quite uncomfortable for a while.

"I don't know if I pull off the country look so well."

"I think you don't know how well you do pull off the country look."

"You are just being nice."

I laugh. *"So I go from asshole to nice?"*

"A moment of relapse in character."

I laugh again. *"Ciara Verbank is quite the comedian and here I thought you were a clothing designer."*

"Jack of many trades."

I lean back on the sofa and kick my feet up. *"I do like your outfit, however, I'd like to see more."*

"More?"

"Yep, give me a personal fashion show. I'll pick out the outfit for tonight."

"I think I can pick out clothes."

"I think you are fully capable of doing so. I am the one that knows where we are going tonight, though."

"You could jump out of character again and be nice. You know, drop me a few hints."

"Cowboy boots are a must. So that means the

cocktail dress you are wearing is a no go." She rolls her eyes. *"C'mon, I want a fashion show!"*

"Seriously?"

"Very seriously."

I give her a nod toward the bedroom. She's so damn cute pouting like a brat. This is going to be fun.

I lost track of the time and now we have to rush to get to tonight's venue. Don't get me wrong, the rush is worth the little show Ciara put on for me. Her last outfit is perfect for tonight. A short jean mini, with a cut-off tank and a short jean jacket - with cowboy boots of course. Ciara pulls off the country look, very well.

"Are you going to tell me where we are going?"

"You'll see, impatient one."

"I hope we are having dinner, I'm famished."

Shit! I didn't think about offering her a snack to hold her over till dinner. I open the mini snack bar and offer her some peanuts, crackers, or chips. *"I promise I'll take you to a nice dinner afterward."*

She reaches for a pack of peanut butter crackers. *"It better be worth the wait."*

CHAPTER 3

"I think it will be." I look out the window as we approach our distinction.

"Gee whiz, you see all those people?"

"I see them. Get used to it, buttercup." She rolls her eyes at my nickname for her. I laugh.

My driver stops out front. *"Wow! We are going to the Grand Ole Opry?"*

"We are!"

"That's really cool. Now, I get the cowboy boots."

How has she not figured out who I am? I like that she doesn't know in a way. I am recognizing everywhere I go. This is a nice change for once.

I wait for my security to open the door. Before we get out, I turn to Ciara. *"I need you to stay with Victoria. No matter what, Ciara."*

"Won't I be with you?"

"You'll be with Victoria for a while. I have to see Cynthia."

We get out and my team keeps the fans away. Once we are inside, I go with Cynthia and Victoria takes Ciara to her seat. Ciara is about to figure out who I am.

"Took you long enough. Christ, Jasper you about had me scrabbling for an excuse for your whereabouts."

"You know I would never miss this."

"Yeah, but we have no time. You have to be on stage, now."

"Time for what? I got this."

I listen to the announcement. *"Ladies and gentlemen, let's welcome back to the stage our very own Jasper Collins!"*

Before I go on stage, I grab a guitar from one of my team members. I told him ahead of time that's all I'd need tonight. I walk out and wave to the fans. I spot Ciara and her eyes are big.

"How are you all doing tonight?" I wait until the claps die down. *"This is my fifth time on this stage and each time, it's still an honor to be here. I want to start with a song I wrote last month called Roots. Let me know what you think."*

I started to sing a song I had written out on the road. I look right at Ciara to see her reaction. It's about a small-town, country boy sticking to his roots. I purposely picked the song because I knew she would have already seen my ranch. I thought maybe if she heard it, she might know I'm serious about seeing where our relationship might go.

I'm not scared to admit I'm a player. Women throw themselves at me daily, so it is easy to get my needs met. I haven't been in a relationship in five years. I didn't want to be in one. My focus has been on making music and singing for whoever wants to hear me. Then out of the blue, I got a call from Millie Verbank about dating her granddaughter. She gave me all the details and I sat on it for about a week. I thought to myself, why the hell not give it a shot. I have nothing to lose by trying out a relationship. Over the course of the months of waiting for my month, I got more and more excited about a real relationship. If it doesn't work out, I can go back to being the player I am known for. No harm in trying.

When the song ends people are on their feet, cheering and clapping. I look right at Ciara and she seems in awe. I smile and wink at her. I wonder if she figured out who I am yet.

I speak to the audience. *"By the sounds in this room, this song might be a hit! I think I need to take it to the Studio."*

I sang three more songs and did some talking in between before leaving the stage. The crowd is mingling around in the lobby, hoping to get an autograph or a picture. I don't mind doing either as I pass through. My real focus is getting back to my new girlfriend. I do owe her a dinner.

Damn, she is hot in cowboy boots! *"Are you ready to get out of here?"*

She looks around at the crowd who still wants my attention. *"Definitely!"*

"Car is out front waiting for us."

My bodyguards get us out of here without hassle. We get in the car and I'm ready for the questions Ciara is going to start asking me. The door is barely shut before she speaks.

"Wow, Mr. Collins, you can sing!"

"So I've been told."

"Are you really on the radio?"

"Have been for years. You really have no idea who I am, do you?"

"By the way you just asked me that, I feel like I should."

"Have you ever heard the song Whiskey, Wranglers, and a Hat?"

"No."

"How about A Cowboy's Dream?"

"Can't say as I know that either."

"Do you even listen to country music?"

"Some, but not much. I like the older stuff. Real country music. Not this pop-country shit."

I get out my cell phone and bring up one of my videos. I hand her the phone to watch.

"*Oh, I love this song! I played Reckless over and over, years ago. I loved this entire album by Steely Barn.*"

"*You are such a pleasant surprise.*"

She watches the video and her jaw drops open. "*You are the singer of Steely Barn?*"

I laugh. "*I am. My band and I started playing together years ago in a steel barn on the ranch. We made it big, as you can see.*"

"*Wow, I feel so dumb! I mean, I should have recognized your face or at least recognized your name.*"

"*My feelings are crushed!*" I laugh again and she pushes my shoulder. "*I enjoyed you not knowing. It was refreshing actually. Honestly, most people thought my real name was Steely Barn. Where they came up with that idea, I don't know. It wasn't until our second album that people realized my name is Jasper Collins.*"

"*I didn't care for your second album.*"

"*Neither did I. It was what you called it earlier, country-pop.*"

"*Yeah, I agree.*"

"*Our record deal was for two albums. I didn't want to stick around for a third. I started my own recording studio so that I could record my music, my way."*

"You write your own songs?"

"All except for the second album. The guys in the band have written a few, but they are mostly mine."

"That's amazing, Jasper."

"Thanks! It was a lot of hard work to get where we are. I wouldn't change it though."

The rest of the ride, Ciara watches a few more videos of the newer stuff. I watch her reactions. I love that she isn't into country-pop because that isn't me. That isn't Steely Barn either.

CHAPTER FOUR
CIARA

I am in complete awe that Jasper is a famous country music singer. I truly feel like a jackass that I didn't place him as Steely Barn. Now that I know who he is, it fits him. No wonder he has a big, cocky head, as he's on the top ten sexy men alive chart. I also know he's known for not being the settling down type. It's been years since I was a fan, he could have changed. I doubt it with what he did to me on the plane. He's sexy as hell and he knows it. I hate to admit it, but it turns me on. I like confident men and he's definitely one of those men.

I give Jasper his phone back when the car stops moving. I raise an eyebrow. He laughs.

"What is this place?"

"The best damn taco shack in Tennessee."

"Okay, if you say so!"

I didn't expect dinner to be coming from a vendor

on wheels. It better be the best damn taco I've ever had or I'll make sure he knows it. I love a good taco.

When Jasper's team does a quick check of the area, we are allowed out without them hovering over us. We go to the taco place on wheels and I look over the menu while Jasper chit-chats with the worker. He doesn't even have to tell the guy his order. I can't decide between the original taco or a pulled pork taco. Both sound delicious.

"Have you decided yet?"

"I have it narrowed down to two."

"Get them both. I got two," he says winking at me.

"I'll have an original soft taco and a pulled pork taco."

"My favorite!"

"Which one?"

"You'll see. You better get a drink."

"I'll have a Margarita," I joke.

He just raises an eyebrow at me. For some reason, I wasn't allowed to have a drink on my flight. I'm wondering by the way he looked at me if that means the entire month.

I end up getting a soda and so does he. It doesn't take long at all for our food to be ready. We sit at a wooden picnic bench. He shows me his pulled pork taco before taking a big bite. I smile and start with mine too. I like this lighter side to him. He seems more relaxed. It's good to take a break from being so cocky.

"Good right?"

"Oh my, God, yes!"

"Do you always moan when something tastes good?"

I lick my lips. *"Maybe!"*

"I like moans, but usually in a different situation."

There's the guy I met earlier today. I ignore his comment by eating. I'm not going to feed his ego so that means I need better control of my taste buds or whatever makes me moan when I eat.

After we ate and we're heading back to the ranch, Jasper asked me to join him for a fire out on the back patio. I was ready to unwind for the night, but I told him sure. When we came out, he gave me a blanket to wrap around my shoulders. He got the fire going and then asked if I wanted a hot drink. I was tempted to say a glass of wine would be nice, but I decided against it. I told him I was fine. He told me he was going in to get a coffee for himself. I sat back and watched the flames. I really started to relax. Sitting around a little fire isn't something I do very often. I forgot how much I like the smell of wood burning.

Jasper comes back out to join me. He sat a tray down on a little table off to the side. He makes himself a cup.

"I made extra in case you changed your mind."

"It does smell good."

"Please, help yourself if you'd like some."

I made a cup and we sat here in silence for a bit. It wasn't until I heard howling off in the distance that I spoke.

"What was that?" I ask, sitting up in my chair.

"Probably a coyote. Don't worry, it's far away."

"It doesn't sound far away."

"It echoes out here in the open. Country life is different from living in a city. You'd be amazed at the sounds you'll hear out here."

"As long as they stay out there, wherever out there is, I'm good."

"I won't let them get you."

"Can I ask you something?"

"Sure!"

"Why the no drink rule on the plane?"

CHAPTER 4

"I don't drink."

"Oh."

Jasper didn't offer any details on why he doesn't drink. So I have no idea why I can't. I'm not a huge drinker either, but a glass of wine with dinner is nice at times. Or even to de-stress after a long day. I'm not going to push the issue. Maybe he'll tell me more eventually about his issue with it. It could be nothing more than he simply doesn't like the taste of alcoholic drinks. I'm too tired to think about it now.

We sat here for quite some time. Both of us are enjoying the quiet and the warm fire. I'm actually ready to crash, but I don't want to be rude. It's been a long day, though.

"I hadn't realized how late it's getting."

Thankfully he brought up how late it is. *"Yeah, I'm getting ready to crash."*

"Mornings come early around here."

"I'm not a fan of mornings."

Jasper stands up from his chair and offers me his hand. I didn't think he'd actually help me get out of the Adirondack style chair and I crashed into his chest. His eyes search mine. He has really nice eyes to go with his whole sex appeal. I thought he was about to kiss me. I was a little relieved when he didn't. I'm still a tiny bit upset at him from earlier today. Although I gotta admit, I am a little curious, too.

Jasper walks me to my bedroom. *"If you need anything, I'm right across the hallway."*

"Okay."

When he leaned in to kiss me, I was a bit surprised, but I let him. Holy hell, the man can kiss. It was an extremely heartfelt kind of kiss.

"If I'm not around in the morning, ask Victoria, she'll know where to find me."

"Okay."

"Good night, buttercup."

"Night, Jasper."

I go into my room and shut the door. I fan my face with my hand. That kiss was nothing like I thought it'd be. I didn't think he'd be that gentle. I thought he'd be more dominant like Kaiden. Although, Kaiden can be passionate too. Ugh! This might be a tough month to get through. I'm trying to be good and not have sex with any more men I meet!

I get some pajamas from my luggage. I thought about taking a shower to get the smoke smell off me, but honestly, I'm tired and really want nothing but sleep. I change my clothes and get into bed.

CHAPTER FIVE
JASPER

Day one down and in the books for having a girlfriend. Even though it's only been one day, I'm delighted to have met Ciara. She really is a breath of fresh air. She played it cool when she finally knew who I was, and I really like that about her. Maybe she isn't all starstruck because she has quite the name for herself. I am not going to lie, I looked her up before I placed my bid to date her. I knew she had a decent reputation before going ahead.

I got up early to help out around the ranch. I really like getting back to my roots when I'm home. I get up and start the day with the ranch help by having breakfast with them out in the bunkhouse. We spend the time together catching me up on what's been happening around here. Then when our stomachs are full, we get to work. By six we all are ready to work until lunch break. Today, I am helping Butch with the cattle. We need to bring them down off the hill so that he and I can repair the fence. A couple of days before I got home a storm came through with high winds and it knocked some of the fencing loose. I don't care to be losing any cattle. I'm a little pissed it's been down two days. Someone was slacking on their duties. Fencing is one of the first things to check after such a strong storm surge. I don't like to call people out in front of others, so once I have time later, I'll pull Garret aside. I won't be firing him, but he'll get a warning not to slack again.

Before I left with Butch, I informed Victoria to stay at the house. She is going to be my eyes on Ciara until I make it back. I also called Cynthia to bring Ciara a nice breakfast since my kitchen help is on vacation this week. Cynthia told me it was no problem at all and for me not to worry. Just get my work done so that I can spend time with my newfound girlfriend. It's extremely weird to hear someone say I have a girlfriend. It did put a smile on my face, though.

It wasn't until just before lunch when I really got a taste of what it's like to have a girlfriend in my life again. Cynthia texted me telling me she was taking Ciara with her to town. I trust my boys to protect Ciara and I know Victoria will keep a good eye on her, but if something were to happen on my watch I would kick myself in the ass. I stayed working, but Ciara was on my mind the entire time. I sent a few texts asking if things were alright. Cynthia got a kick out of me worrying so much. She's not used to me caring about someone other than my close friends and of course my mom. Hell, I'm not used to this sort of behavior, either.

When the workday is done, we all head in. The fence is repaired, the cattle are back in the field on the hill and the animals are all fed. It was a great workday all-in-all. I am very much looking forward to seeing Ciara and spending some alone time with her. However, when I get to the house there is a spread of food laid out for the entire crew. I should have known what Cynthia was up to when she said she was going into town. She loves cooking for the boys and when she does, it's a big display.

I look around for Ciara. *"Relax, big guy, she's getting some food from the kitchen."*

"Christ, there's more!"

I am just about to head into the house to find her when she comes outside, carrying a big pot of corn on the cob. One of the boys sees her and takes it from her. She spots me and smiles. My eyes travel her entire body. Damn, she looks hot in daisy-dukes, a flannel tied in front, and cowboy boots. I'd like to strip her down, article by article until she stands before me naked. I would cherish her body inch-by-inch - slowly, taking my time to learn her body language.

"Hi!"

I snap out of my sexual thoughts. *"Evening."*

"I hope you're hungry. Cynthia went a little crazy."

I look at the table full of food. It's seafood galore - shrimp, crab legs, lobster tails, and some kind of fish. The side dishes aren't missing either. Salads, corn on the cob, and lemon bread.

"I think I can eat, but we better hurry before the boys eat everything on that table."

Ciara and I fill our plates with food along with everyone else. We all eat together at a table the girls put together. I peek out of the corner of my eye at Ciara when she moans. I'm trying hard to ignore her sweet sounds. I eventually lean into her space and whisper in her ear.

"You are making me hard."

She puts a hand to her mouth and coughs, then has

CHAPTER 5

a sip of lemonade. When the shock of what I said wore off, she whispered back, *"I thought men only had to undo their jeans at the dinner table because they eat too much."*

I laugh. Everyone at the table is looking at us. I cough once. I wait until they go back to eating before I reply.

"I guess you don't moan while eating around them."

"Maybe I do, maybe I don't. I'd tell you, but it would almost be like kissing and telling."

I laugh again. This time the table minds their own business. I watch Ciara suck the butter off her fingers. Eating with this girl might become impossible. I can't be getting hard every damn meal. I do my best to ignore how badly I want her. I'm trying my hardest to be good.

Cynthia gets my mind off Ciara. *"Jasper, I called the band this afternoon, they are all set to meet here tomorrow night."*

"Great, what time are we heading out?"

"Midnight." I nod my head.

Ciara looks at me. *"Where are you going at midnight?"*

"We are leaving Tennessee. I have to play at a bar

in West Virginia, then a concert in Ohio this weekend."

"Oh!"

"We'll be taking my tour bus."

"I see."

"I hope you are okay in a confined space?"

"I've been on Hawk Evans' bus and did fine."

Her bringing up another man sort of bothers me. I try not to let that show. Being a jealous boyfriend could make me look bad. I don't want her to think I'm a bigger jerk than she thought from the plane.

"After dinner, do you want a tour of the ranch?"

"I thought you'd never ask."

We won't be spending our entire time together out on the road. We'll be bouncing back and forth between the ranch and the bus. I want her to be comfortable with both.

CHAPTER SIX
CIARA

Once we were done eating, we both helped take the leftovers inside. I guess the rule is if someone cooks for the crew, the crew is on washing dishes duty. The guys don't even seem to mind. I think Jasper is lucky, it seems his crew is like family to him.

Jasper and I have been walking around his ranch. So far, I like the horses the most. I have never been on a horse before. I am a bit terrified of them. Jasper did ask me if I wanted to ride tomorrow and I told him maybe. He told me if I fear them, they will know it. How I don't know. I guess it's one of their senses. I could stay up all night stressing over it, but there is no need. Jasper assured me that there isn't much to it. I want to give it a shot, I am game to try something that is important to him.

After our walk, we came out to the back patio to

relax by the fire as we did last night. I think I could get used to this. I feel comfortable here.

"Sorry I worked all day."

"It's no problem. I enjoyed being with the girls and making all that food."

"Did you notice anyone in town following you?"

"Not that I'm aware of." This question makes me nervous. *"Should I have?"*

"Victoria said she saw someone watching you at the store."

"I didn't notice. I didn't see anyone I know either."

Jasper reaches out his hand and I put my palm to his. He laces our fingers together. *"I don't want to make you nervous when in public. My team won't let anyone get to you and neither will I."*

At least Jasper has people watching out for me, but what happens if this person isn't caught and next month comes along, who will protect me then? I wish I knew who this person was. Grams called me earlier and told me there are no updates. The police still have nothing. At this rate, my stalker could get away with vandalism. I hope that isn't true. What is stopping this person or persons from going after the people I care about. Lucky Grams has a bodyguard. It gives me a little comfort that she isn't alone. She doesn't have a

CHAPTER 6

full team of men as Jasper does, but at least she has someone.

"You got quiet on me."

"I was just thinking about Grams. I'm glad she has someone who goes everywhere with her."

"I'm glad she does, too." Jasper sits upright in his chair. *"Don't move."*

Jasper puts a finger to his lips, as well. I twisted in my seat even though he told me not to move. My eyes get big as they land on a dog. I don't remember him having a dog. I get nervous when I remember him telling me last night about coyotes. Oh shit! I don't move another muscle.

"Ciara, I need you to get up very slowly and go into the house."

I inch my way to the end of the seat, not taking my eyes off the coyote. I really don't wanna be eaten tonight. I swear the closer I get to the edge of my seat, the coyote takes a step closer to me.

"I'm not going to let him near you, but I really need you to go to the house."

I get to my feet, even though he told me to go slow, my body reacts. I start running for the door. When my hand touches the door handle, I hear a gunshot. Holy hell! Did Jasper shoot it? I don't stop to look. When I get behind the glass French door, I look outside. Jasper has his phone in one hand and a pistol in the other. Where the hell did he have that? I open the door. He looks at me over his shoulder.

"Is it dead?"

"Yes."

I step outside. *"Did you shoot it?"*

"Yes."

"Oh."

"I have to call Butch to clean this up."

"Can I see it?"

"Really?"

"Ya, I wanna see what wanted to eat me for dinner."

"It's not pretty."

We walk over to where the dead animals lay after he calls Butch. It isn't pretty as he said, but damn it is bigger up close. I don't recall seeing coyotes at the zoo when I went with Lincoln. Butch comes riding up on a four wheeler.

"Nice shot," he says to Jasper.

"Have you seen any other wolves around?"

Wolf? I tell Jasper I'm going to the house. I've seen enough. I am a little overwhelmed. I have a stalker after me and now a wolf that wanted to eat me. I make my way to my room and sit on the bed. Sleep might not come so easily tonight as it did last night. I fall back onto the bed and stare up at the ceiling.

I don't really know how long I am alone before Jasper comes to my door.

"Are you alright?"

I sit up on the bed and burst into tears. These are not a few tears here and there, it's a full out cry. Japer comes and kneels down on the floor in front of me and puts his arms around me. I put my forehead on his shoulder. He runs his hand down the back of my hair.

"I'm sorry," I manage to say through my sniffles.

Jasper lifts my head to look at me. *"Don't be sorry for expressing emotions. I'm sorry you had to witness me shooting my gun."*

"I've never been around wildlife or guns before."

"I figured as much."

"Can you teach me?"

"How to use a gun?"

"Yes!"

"Yeah, we can do that tomorrow. We better get some rest."

"I think I'm ready to crash."

"Are you sure you are alright?"

"I think so."

"If you need me, I'll be across the hall."

"Okay."

Jasper leans in and kisses my forehead. *"Good night, Ciara."*

"Good night, Jasper."

Once Jasper has left my room, I get changed into a little nightie and crawl into bed. I roll onto my side and close my eyes. Flashes of my destroyed shop come into my mind, then the saying on my apartment door about karma. I roll over and bury my head under a pillow. The image of the wild wolf staring at me comes into my mind. I keep tossing and turning. It's causing me slight anxiety. I throw the blankets back and get out of bed. I go into the bathroom and splash my face with some cool water. It doesn't really do anything for me. When I get back out to the bedroom, I take one look at the bed and then toward the door. Jasper's bedroom door is wide open. Without another thought, I go to his room and peek my head inside. I gasp when he comes walking out from his bathroom wet and naked. I inhale a breath when he spots me. He stops moving and looks at me.

"Can I sleep in here tonight?"

"Yes."

CHAPTER SEVEN
JASPER

I come out of the shower without drying off or wrapping a towel around me. That's nothing unusual for me. What's unusual is having a woman in my house, peeking into my room. I don't have women in my house, most of my sexual encounters are in a hotel room or dressing room. I don't even have ladies in my bus. My bus and home are my private places. One-night stands don't need to be in my personal space.

She asked if she could sleep in my room tonight and I told her, yes, but she hasn't entered my room yet. I walk over to where Ciara is frozen in place and take her by the hand, leading her to the bed. I pull back the blankets. She gets under the blankets. I walk over to the other side and get into bed.

"You're not putting clothes on?"

"I sleep naked, buttercup."

"*Oh!*"

I silently laugh as she rolls onto her side, putting her back to me. I am tempted to roll to my side and put an arm around her, but I don't want to make her uncomfortable. Plus, snuggling isn't something I do. I need to be a gentleman and let her get some sleep.

Ciara can't seem to get comfortable. She keeps tossing and turning. With everything going on in her life, it must make it difficult to keep your mind clear. Me having to shoot the wolf tonight in front of her probably didn't help.

"Is my bed uncomfortable?" I ask to try and take her mind off of whatever is bothering her.

"No, I'm sorry. My mind just won't shut off. I can go back to my room if I'm keeping you awake."

"I can help you relax, but I'll have to touch you."

"Touch me how?" She asks, rolling onto her back.

"Like this."

I reach over and put my hand on her stomach and then lightly trace my fingers up between her breasts. *"Think about nothing other than what I'm about to do to your body. If you want me to stop, just say so."*

I keep moving my fingers higher up until they reach her lips. I run my finger over her bottom lip, then her top lip. I let my knuckles lightly graze her cheek before I lean in and kiss her. Her hand comes to my face as she accepts my mouth and deepens the kiss. I trail my fingertips back down her body to her inner thigh. Breaking the kiss, I watch her expression as the moonlight gives me just enough light to see her face. I move her panties off to the side and tease her clit. When she widens her legs further apart, I know she wants me to go further. I could give her pleasure with just my fingers alone, but adding my tongue and mouth will give her a better orgasm. An orgasm that will put her right to sleep. So, I continue playing with her then bend over her chest, sucking a nipple between my lips. I feel her body relax and that is when I move my mouth lower. Her nails dig into the skin of my back as I lick her lower lips. She tastes better than I imagined.

My fingers, my mouth, and my tongue bring her pleasure. Her moans are ten times better than when she eats. When her thighs clutch my head, I feel them trembling. Her orgasm is right there hanging off the side of a cliff. I suck her clit harder, my fingers graze the ribbed area faster. Her breathing is labored as she falls over the edge. I don't stop what I'm doing to her body until she's finished.

I move back up her body and kiss her. *"Goodnight, Ciara."*

"What about you," she asks, trying to reach for my erection.

"I'm fine, go to sleep," I say moving to my back on my side of the bed.

Ciara moves over and puts her head in the space between my chest and shoulder. Her hand goes to my hardness. *"That doesn't seem fair."*

I remove her hand and interlock our fingers. *"What I just did was for you. Sleep, we have a busy day tomorrow."*

It doesn't take Ciara long at all to fall asleep. For me on the other hand, sleep isn't coming as easily. I am hard as fuck. I could have let Ciara take care of my needs, but it wasn't about me tonight. It was about her. The media has called me selfish or ignorant when it comes to commitment. They know nothing about who I am. They only know the side of me that I let them see. I care about many people. Once I let someone into my life, those people become very important to me. Those are the people that know I am the opposite of selfish.

Ciara moves in her sleep, covering my body more with hers. Her moving doesn't help my erection at all. It also makes it more difficult for me to slip out from underneath her to take care of my problem. She mumbles something, but I couldn't quite make out what she had said.

I switch my mind to something other than wanting to wake Ciara and fucking her until the sun comes up. Otherwise, I am not going to get a wink of sleep. I start thinking about teaching Ciara how to shoot a gun. I can picture it now, me standing behind her and showing her how to aim. Moving in close enough so her back is touching my front. Having her ear close to my lips as I give her instructions. Her little whimpers escaping from her throat as she tries to concentrate on my instructions instead of the sexual chemistry between us. She moans when my hands begin to crest her body and slip into the front of her shorts.

My attempt to get my mind off of the erection I have, failed. My cock is throbbing. I really need to take care of it or I'm not getting any sleep tonight. I slowly slip out from underneath Ciara. When I stand from the bed, she blinks her eyes open. I bend over the bed and whisper.

"I'm just using the bathroom. I'll be right back."

Her eyes close as she rolls over to her side of the bed. I don't even think she fully woke up. Which is good. She really needs a good night's rest. I go into the bathroom and shut the door. I waste no time. I grip my manhood and start stroking its length and girth.

All I have to do is think about the things I want to do to Ciara's body. I get more turned on than I already was. It doesn't take long for the release to come. After I let the orgasm pass, I clean up and head back to bed, hoping that sleep will come easily now.

CHAPTER EIGHT
CIARA

When it's seven in the morning and you wake up to an empty bed, you have to wonder if the person you slept next to got any sleep at all. I knew Jasper said he gets up early, but how early? It was after midnight when I came to his room last night.

I slipped out of Jasper's bed and went across the hall to my room so that I could shower and get ready for the day. Seven in the morning is early for me. I usually sleep until at least nine. While I was showering, I thought about last night and the way Jasper got my mind to shut off. I like his way of distracting me. He can do that to my body any night. You won't see me arguing with him.

Being on this ranch with him has shown me a different side to him. He's not a cocky jerk when he's here. Maybe I'm seeing the real him and the way he acted on the plane was just a stunt he pulled to see if he could get away with it. I don't know for sure what it is, but I like Jasper, even the cocky side to him.

"Oh good, you're awake. I got the horses all saddled up and ready to go."

"You aren't wasting any time this morning."

"You should never waste daylight on a ranch."

I finish putting my boots on. *"I'm ready."*

I follow Jasper out to the front door and he picked up a bag before going outside. Two horses stand side-by-side tied to the railing of the porch. He wasn't kidding when he said he had the horses ready to go.

"You are riding, Texas Tornado."

"That sounds safe."

"He was just a baby when I got him. I thought he'd be a heller, so I gave him a name I thought would be fitting. Turns out, I was wrong. He's as gentle as a cool breeze on a sunny day."

I laugh as I touch his face. *"Nothing wrong with a cool breeze on a sunny day, huh, Texas Tornado?"*

"Here let me give you a boost up."

Jasper helps me get on the horse's back. He then tells me he forgot something in the house. I was nervous he left me alone on a horse. To calm myself, I talked to my horse and rubbed his neck. When Jasper comes out he unties the horses, then gets on his horse.

I notice he has his guitar in a case strapped to his back.

"Who are you riding?"

"Rocky Mountain Man."

"Did you name him, as well?"

"I didn't. He came with the name."

Jasper gives me a quick lesson on how to ride. By the time we hit the trail, I was doing just fine. I wasn't scared or nervous anymore. Riding a horse is peaceful.

Jasper led me to a place on the land where he said he comes to get away from everyone. He said it's here he'd come to write songs or just sing and play his guitar. He laid out a blanket he had in the bag, then he showed me he packed us muffins and a thermos of coffee. We ate together as he told me about a few songs he wrote out here. Most of them I knew because they were on his first album.

After a while, Jasper gets out his guitar and starts playing. I lay on my side with my head resting on his thigh near his knee. Jasper has dirty blond hair that isn't cut short like the other guys. His is a tad bit longer. It reminds me of Keith Urban's hairstyle. I can't picture him with shorter hair. His blue eyes are captivating. If you stare into them long enough it's like you can see into his soul. If he doesn't let you see them, then they are mysterious. I watch his dirty blond hair blow in the slight breeze as he strums his guitar and sings. I bite my bottom lip and then smile. He really is amazing when he sings.

"You are cute when you have that sparkle in your eye."

"You are handsome when you are relaxed."

He strums his guitar and I smile when he begins to play *Reckless*. I love having my own personal concert. It's ten times better that it's in one of his favorite places to play. I thought Jasper was sexy as fuck on the plane, but witnessing him in his own element is even sexier. I can't deny it, I'm very attracted to him.

When the song ends, I sit up and lean into his space. Our lips are only inches apart. I comb my fingernails through his beard. His hand comes to my cheek before he leans the rest of the way in and we kiss.

When our lips part, I take his guitar from him and set it off to the side. I then straddle his lap and kiss him again. I want to be with him. I have a hunger for Jasper Collins and I need to feed it. As our tongues

CHAPTER 8

intertwine, I take the hem of his shirt and start lifting it. He grabs it from the back and helps me remove it. He unties the knot I put in the front of my thin flannel shirt then unbuttons it. His hands fill with my breasts once my shirt is open. I finish removing my shirt and discard my bra. I moan when his lips are all over my chest, kissing my skin ever so lightly. I let him know how much I want him by grinding my lower body against his lap. I reach for his belt.

"Are you sure you are ready to cross that line?"

"Yes."

"Ciara, I'm not always..."

When he pauses too long, I ask, *"Not always, what?"*

"I'm not always gentle and lovey-dovey."

"I already figured you weren't." I undo his belt as I kiss his neck. *"Are you going to allow me to be in charge?"*

I yelp when he quickly flips our bodies and I become pinned underneath him. *"Not today, buttercup."*

His mouth is on mine before I can reply. I don't mind at all. I want Jasper to have control. I want whatever it is he wants to give me. I already figured out he's a dominant man just like Kaiden. I can't wait to see just how dominating he really is.

Jasper pulls my boots off, then undoes my shorts, yanking them off. His blue eyes wander around my naked body as he finishes getting his jeans open. I lick my lips as his manhood is freed from the confinement of his jeans. He snickers and brings me to a sitting position. He holds his shaft and strokes it. I remove his hand and replace it with mine. I love the hissing sound that he makes when I suck the head of his cock between my lips. Men like Jasper only give you enough control to pleasure their manhood until they take control back. How they can switch on and off for a moment is something I haven't figured out yet. Maybe giving the woman control for a brief moment is part of the whole dominant game. Whatever it is, it really doesn't much matter. I'm learning I like the whole Dom/sub thing in the bedroom. It turns me on just thinking about it.

Before I can finish Jasper off, he takes his cock from my mouth. He kisses me and nudges my body to lay back. His kiss becomes more aggressive - more demanding. I gasp when his cock abruptly enters me. My body reacts to the intrusion by stiffening. It takes me a minute to relax and when it does, the pleasure of his manhood takes over. My body accepts all of him and I become a withering mess beneath him. Holy hell, the orgasm that rips through me takes my breath away. I don't even have time to recover when he flips my body over and I'm on all fours. He isn't gentle when he pounds into me from behind. His thrusting is fast and hard. I reward him by cumming again. He rewards me by pulling out and marking my back. I collapsed to the ground on my stomach with him on top of me. He rolls off of me and we both catch our breaths. Jasper didn't dominate my body by spanking me, but he was one hundred percent in charge of our orgasms.

CHAPTER NINE
JASPER

Ciara and I left my ranch three days ago. We pulled into West Virginia yesterday. I had a solo gig at a bar last night, then we got back on the bus and headed to Ohio for the weekend. It was late when we pulled in. We will be here for the next two nights and I'm a bit nervous for Ciara. Nobody seems to know who is stalking her and seeing that there are over two-hundred-thousand people here this weekend, it makes it easy for whoever to blend in if he followed her here. My entire security team is with me, but with a crowd this large it will be difficult for them to notice every little thing around us. Ciara is more adventurous than she thinks she is. Keeping her locked up safely on the bus isn't going to happen. She's going to want to see what is going on. This weekend is nothing but a huge party.

I go to the back of the bus and peek in on her. She's still sleeping soundly. I hate to wake her, but I need to tell her I have to leave for a bit.

I put a knee on the bed and lean over, kissing Ciara on the cheek. Her eyes don't open but a moan escapes past her lips.

"I have to go to a meeting in a few minutes."

"Ugh! What time is it?"

"Nine."

She rolls into her back and peeks one eye open. *"What kind of meeting?"*

"My stage crew needs to meet with the coordinators and I need to find out when I'm playing."

"Do you need me to go with you?"

"I want to show you something."

"Okay."

I pull back the covers and Ciara's naked body looks tempting. If I didn't have this meeting, I would take full advantage of having her naked in my bed. The last three days we've had a lot of sex. I have an addictive personality and I'm fully aware I'm addicted to her. I could very easily forget everything and do nothing else but have sex with Ciara all day, every day.

Before we leave the bedroom area, she puts a robe

on. Ciara comes out to the front of the bus with me. I open the door and show her outside. She steps off my bus with her jaw wide open.

"Holy hell, that's a lot of people."

"This weekend is going to be crazy. If I'm not around, you have to stick with my guys."

"Why are there so many people?"

"It's called the Jamboree in the Hills. It's three days packed full of country music non-stop. It started yesterday."

"I've never seen this many people camping in one place before. This is going to be fun."

I go back inside and grab a baseball cap and a pair of shades. Ciara had followed me back inside.

"I shouldn't be gone more than an hour. Help yourself to whatever you want to eat."

"I'll probably shower."

"Whatever you do, please don't leave this bus. We can wander around when I get back."

Ciara rolls her eyes at me. Apparently she is forgetting that someone destroyed her shop and someone was watching her at the grocery store. It isn't too difficult to find out my concert dates. Anyone with half a brain can figure out where I am at. Since it was in the tabloids that Ciara is dating me, it's easy to find out where she's at as well.

I give Ciara a kiss goodbye. I ask her nicely to stay put until I get back. With music jamming and partying going on, I know how tempting it can be to be part of the action.

My plan today was to chill with Ciara while listening to other bands playing, have a cookout with my crew, and to lay as low as possible. But once I got to the meeting, they asked if I'd go on today. I'm not supposed to play until tomorrow night. Apparently one of the bands is stuck in Kentucky with no way here. There are no flights and two of their buses are broke down. I'm not one to say no, so my band agreed to play twice. I'm playing at six tonight and nine tomorrow tonight. Instead of wandering around chillin' with Ciara, my band is at my campsite going over our playlist for today and one for tomorrow night. Ciara seems cool with it. I know there's still plenty of time to be with Ciara, but I really wanted her to experience this day as a fan and not a girlfriend of Jasper Collins. Hell I was looking forward to being just a fan today. Many of my fellow country stars are on stage today.

Ciara bumps her shoulder to mine. *"It's pretty*

cool to see how you and your band pick songs. I can't wait to see you guys play."

"We should be about done. Wanna sneak off for a couple of hours?"

"By sneaking off, do you mean just the two of us?"

"My guys will be close by, but you won't notice them."

"Hell yeah, let's do it!"

I tell everyone Ciara and I are going to check out. I get my ball cap and sunglasses. Ciara gets her cowboy hat to wear and her sunglasses as well. We hold hands as we begin to leave the campsite. We act as if we are nobodies as we mingle in with the crowd heading to the music.

"I've been playing at this jamboree for the last six years. I swear the crowd gets bigger and the party gets rowdier every year."

"It's got to be exciting for you to play for so many people."

"It is. It's also easy to fall into the party with the fans."

"You mean drinking with them?"

"Yep. The first two years I was drunk all weekend."

CHAPTER 9

"Now you don't drink?"

"Nope, I haven't had a drink in three years. Alcohol just about ruined me. I don't want anything to do with it."

"That's why I'm not allowed to drink."

"Yep!"

I don't go into many details about my drinking and the past. I don't talk about those days very much. I prefer to leave those days buried where they belong. I have come a long way to stay sober and I plan on staying that way.

I took Ciara to the VIP section and we listened to a few bands play before we headed back to the campsite. I had to meet up with the boys and get a change of clothes. We all went down to the stage as a group. I left Ciara in the VIP section with three of my bodyguards. I wanted her to be stage side with Cynthia, but she wanted to be out front to feel the crowd. I only allowed it because she agreed to stay put. I also felt better knowing the band member's wives or girlfriends were there, as well. If Ciara and I end up together, she will become friends with some of the ladies, I hope.

Everything seems to be going great until I see my drummer's girlfriend, Melissa hand Ciara a solo cup.

Melissa is a drinker, so I can only imagine what's in the cup. Ciara accepts it - she better hope it's only Kool-Aid.

CHAPTER TEN
CIARA

I am having the best time hanging out in the VIP area with all of Steely Barn's wives or girlfriends, watching my boyfriend perform on stage. I never saw myself as being a groupie, but this is a lot of fun. It's one thing that I am dating the hottest country star, but you feed off the energy from the crowd. I've never been one to go to concerts, but I could do this more often. You scream, dance, and sing along with Jasper. This is so exciting. The hour and a half went by so fast. I am having fun and would love to stay to see who is on stage next. I hope Jasper will want to stay too. Otherwise, the fun is over.

I quickly learn that I don't get to stay as Victoria tells me it's time to go. I am a little upset that I don't even get a choice. She takes hold of my arm near my elbow, ready to lead me out of the area and I yank my arm free. I told her I wanted to stay longer. She shakes her head no. I make my stance. She doesn't get to tell me what I can and cannot do.

I watch as she walks off and smiled. I finished drinking whatever Melissa gave me, proud that I stood up for myself.

Melissa tells me she is leaving and fills my solo cup up before she leaves. Me being proud of myself fades quickly as I see Jasper coming toward me. By his expression, he isn't happy I didn't go with Victoria. The tone of his voice, he is pissed off.

"Do you mind telling me what the hell you are doing?"

Now, I am pissed. He doesn't have the right to talk to me like I am a child getting scolded. *"I am a grown woman, I don't think I need to answer to you. Your security team doesn't get to tell me what I am allowed to do. I am not ready to go. I want to stay and listen to more music."*

"Stay if you want, but don't plan on sleeping in my bed tonight."

"Maybe I won't sleep in your bed ever again."

"Enjoy your fucking drink."

"Are you fucking serious? I'm not allowed to have lemonade? What the fuck is your problem?"

"Just lemonade? Enjoy the shows."

I watch as he walks off. I might have flipped him

off behind his back. He stops and talks to Victoria. He can take her back with him. I don't need a fucking babysitter. I smile when I see her leaving with him. I drink down half the glass of my drink.

It isn't long before the next band starts to play. I only stick around for about half of it. The fun went away as soon as Jasper was being an asshole. I finished off my drink before I left and wandered through the crowd as I tried to find my way back to the campsite. There are a helluva lot of people here. It isn't difficult to find the camping area but remembering where we were exactly isn't that easy. I didn't need to worry about it after all because I wasn't left alone. Jasper did have one of his guys babysitting me after all.

I look at his bodyguard, and ask, *"Where is your boss?"*

"I don't know, ma'am, I was with you."

"Don't you have communication to find out?"

"Give me a second."

We keep walking and he gets on the phone with someone. I glance around at all the campers having a good time. This jamboree is like one huge party. I bet this is what it must have felt like to be at Woodstock. I've watched old videos of it and it's exactly what it reminds me of.

"Jasper is on his bus."

"That's where you are taking me, right?"

"Yes, ma'am."

We only have to walk another five minutes or so. When I get to Jasper's bus, the door is locked. I bang on the door, but he doesn't answer. Fuck him! He can be mad at me for whatever reason and sit on his bus pouting like a child. I see everyone else in the band over on another site. It's probably one of the band member's buses. I am not going to keep banging on the door to see what the hell jasper's problem is, so I go over and join them.

I find Melissa and ask her if I can have another drink. She makes a helluva good lemonade. She raises her eyebrow at me as if I am crazy that I asked her for another drink. Her attitude has completely changed.

"Jasper chewed me a new one when we got back for giving you drinks."

"Why?"

"Because of the alcohol in the drink."

Honestly, I had no idea there was alcohol in the drink. It tastes like plain old lemonade to me. *"That's insane, I am a big girl and can decide if I want a drink or not."*

"Jasper and Grant got into a big fight about it. I

am new to the group, so I had no idea I wasn't supposed to give you a drink."

"Well, you know what, Melissa, I am new, too. I am not going to have Jasper dictate what I can and can't do. I want another drink."

Her eyes get big at me asking for more. She can be a puppet or she can have the freedom to do as she wishes. The choice is hers. She tilts her head to the right, pointing me in the direction of the drink she had. I think twice about pissing Jasper off more, but in the end, I do what I want. I have asked him twice about drinking and he didn't want to elaborate on it, so he can kiss my ass. Just because he has a past with drinking doesn't mean I do. Just because we are in this month-long relationship doesn't mean he gets to tell me what to do. At least not without an explanation.

I can't begin to tell you how many drinks I have had. Hell, I don't even have a clue as to what time it is. The sun has long passed over the horizon. The party is not winding down at all. I've been hanging out with Jasper's band members and friends while he hasn't come off his bus. If he has, I haven't seen him. I have tried a couple of times to get him to answer the door, but he ignored me. I guess my boyfriend and I are having a fight. I am just going to enjoy this cozy little fire and chill. Hell, this might be where I sleep tonight since the asshole locked me out of his bus. When tomorrow comes I just might get the hell out of here and go home. Dating someone who wants to lock me out is a waste of my time. Maybe I shouldn't wait until tomorrow and leave now. I could, except my purse is on the bus. Damn him!

CHAPTER ELEVEN
JASPER

I was so fucking pissed off at Ciara last night. I gave her one simple rule to follow and she failed. I even gave her a chance to follow my rule and she still went and did her own thing. I didn't ask her to change who she is, I simply said no drinking. I thought by telling her I have been sober three years and drinking just about ruined me would have been enough for her to stay away from alcohol. I seriously thought the relationship we were building meant something to her. I guess I was wrong. Maybe this is why I'm better off being a player. I don't have to tell anyone that I want nothing to do with drinking. I watched as Ciara poured herself another drink when she got back, then another and another. Over the course of four hours, I saw her drink at least four more alcoholic beverages. That was six drinks I know she had. It wasn't until she passed out at the fire that I left my bus. I went out and carried her to bed. The smell of vodka on her breath turned my stomach. I tucked her into bed then slept on the sofa. I don't know how this relationship can go anywhere if she wants to act that way. I know the way I acted last night probably hasn't helped, but I didn't know what else to do. Alcohol cannot be a part of my life. I can't kiss the woman I love and taste the alcohol. It would be too easy to fall back into drinking. I worked too damn hard to be sober. I fought my way out of the bottom of a whiskey bottle to risk falling back into it.

    The first thing I did when I woke up this morning was check on Ciara. She was still sleeping soundly, so I left the bus and went for a walk. I had to clear my mind and figure out if Ciara is worth fighting for. We have a strong sexual connection. I care about her deeply even though we barely know one another. I want to know more about her. I want to continue getting to know her better. I have feelings for the girl that I didn't realize I had until last night. If I didn't have feelings, I would have sent her packing last night. Clearly Ciara and I need to have a serious conversation. If she's not feeling what I'm feeling then there's no point in going further. I'm not going to waste my time nor hers. Spending this time with

Ciara has shown me I want more. I want a real relationship. I'm ready to find a woman and settle down. I am ready to cut back on touring and be on the ranch more.

I headed back to the bus, ready to try and fix my relationship with Ciara. I can't deny I like the girl. Hell, I may even be falling in love with her. When I get back Grant is outside his bus making a cup of coffee. I really laid into him yesterday. I should probably apologize to him.

"*Hey,*" I say.

"*Jasper.*"

"*I'm sorry about yesterday. I had no right yelling at you.*"

"*You're damn right you didn't. Lucky for you I understand your issues with drinking. Melissa on the other hand doesn't and neither does Ciara. It's them you should be saying sorry to.*"

"*I will, to both of them.*"

"*Dude, there's going to come a day that you're not going to be able to control every situation. Some people can be social drinkers and not be alcoholics. If you end up with Ciara you can't tell her she can't drink. You're going to need to find a way to be okay with that.*"

"*Yeah, I know.*"

"I don't think you handled yourself very well by locking Ciara out of the bus. By the looks of it, you might have ruined a good relationship." He nods his head toward my bus. I look.

"Shit!"

"Good luck, buddy."

I call out Ciara's name as I rush over to my bus. She ignores my voice. I don't blame her. Payback for yesterday. She gets in a waiting car as the driver puts her belongings in the trunk. I tell him to stop what he's doing. I get out my wallet and throw him a hundred dollar bill. That works. I go to the back passenger door and try to open it. Ciara locks me out. Again, I don't blame her.

"Ciara, come back to the bus and we can talk about this in private."

"You could have done that yesterday, but you went and pouted like a child and locked me out. Go to hell, asshole."

"Ciara, please give me the chance to explain my actions and fix this." She shakes her head no. I look at the driver. *"Unlock the car."* He shrugs his shoulders. Fucker! I give him another hundred dollars. I open the car door and reach in pulling Ciara from inside. I then pick her up and put her over my shoul-

der, carrying her to the bus. She kicks and screams for me to put her down. *"You can go after you hear me out."* I put Ciara on her ass on the sofa. She tries to make a move for the door, but I block it.

"Let me out, asshole."

"Not until you hear me out, buttercup."

"Stop calling me that!"

"Sit down!" She narrows her eyes at me and crosses her arms over her chest. She is cute when she's angry.

"Hurry up, I want to leave."

"I'm an alcoholic. I started drinking when my father passed away. I didn't know how to handle his death, so I drank nonstop. My drinking nearly cost me my career, my band, and my friendships. It took me a long time to stop drinking. I want nothing to do with it at all."

"Just because you have a problem doesn't mean I do."

"I know that. I'm not concerned about your drinking. I'm worried if you have alcohol lingering in your mouth and I kiss you I'll want a drink. I can't go back to that life."

"You could have told me. I didn't even realize there was alcohol in the lemonade."

"You didn't know you were drinking Blue Whales? Lemonade isn't blue, you know!"

"I thought it was blue raspberry lemonade. You acted like a child. You're the one who shut me out."

"I know, I'm sorry. I handled it all wrong yesterday. I don't want you to go."

"You cannot stop me from having a drink once in a while if we are together."

"I know. I can't fix that overnight, either. I have feelings for you and I'm not ready for us to end."

"I'm not a mind reader."

"I know that. I'm not used to being in a relationship. You make me want to be in one. I'm a work in progress. Please stay."

"Don't ever lock me out again. You embarrassed me in front of all your friends."

"It won't happen again. If it does, I won't stop you from leaving."

"If I'm staying, I need food."

"You don't want makeup sex?"

"Later! I need food first."

I go over to her and crouch down in front of her. I run my fingers along her jaw. *"I'm sorry,"* I say before kissing her cheek.

"Me too."

I turn her face toward mine and kiss her. I have a

lot of making up to do. I really do care about this girl and I don't want to lose her. Not over this. I need to win this woman's heart. I'm already falling for her. I know I'm number seven and there are three more guys after me wanting to love Ciara.

CHAPTER TWELVE
CIARA

Jasper and I went to find some food at one of the food stands. We then walked around for a bit until he was getting recognized too much and was stopped too many times for an autograph. It was cool at first but then it became a little annoying. We just wanted to spend time together since yesterday was such a train wreck. We pretty much have kissed and made up, but we still wanted to be left alone. We ended up coming back to the bus and stayed inside for hours. Once we were in private we really made up with each other. Sex with Jasper is incredible on its own, but add making up into the mix and holy hell it's hotter. Both of us needed a cool shower afterward. I don't think there was an inch of our skin that wasn't covered in sweat. I let him shower first since he needed to talk with his band members and I still needed to catch my breath.

CHAPTER 12

Jasper will be playing his original set. He told me he wants to leave when he's done. I'm good with leaving after his concert. I am looking forward to going back to his ranch.

"Hey!"

"Hey!"

"Are you ready to go?"

"I am. I just need to get my boots on."

"I told the guys we are heading home after the show."

"Are they okay with it?"

"They are. They're ready to get out of here, as well."

I get my boots on, then we meet up with the band outside. We all leave the campsites together as a group. I go to the VIP section with the ladies while the guys go backstage. Jasper wanted me on the side of the stage again, but I refused. I want to experience this from the front. I have his team watching me like a hawk.

Within the next few minutes, Steely Barn comes out on stage. The crowd goes crazy. Women scream Jasper's name. When he steps near the stage edge, women reach for him just to touch him. When he crouches down to give them a high-five a few even grab his private areas. I had no idea women acted in such a way. He immediately stands up and moves away from the crazies. It kinda pisses me off that people actually act that way. Would women like it if I grabbed their husband's or boyfriend's ass or private area? I think not. Jasper gave me a sorry look, but it's not him who should be sorry. He didn't do anything wrong. I am sure he probably didn't mind the groping before I came along, though.

I let it go and enjoy his concert. I want this to be a happy experience. I don't know if I'll get to attend another concert in the time we have left with one another. I am doing just that when an arm comes to rest across my back and hand grips my shoulder. I shrug the arm off me and look to see who touched me. I am shocked. I take a few steps away from him. What the hell is he doing here?

"Jasper Collins is the flavor of the month? When are you going to stop all this nonsense your Grandmother started?"

"What I do with my life is none of your goddamn business. What the hell are you doing here anyway? Never mind, I don't want to know, just please just leave me alone."

I turn and move further away from Hunter. Seriously, what in the hell is he doing here? Honestly, I don't really care. I just want him to stay away from me. I am not so blessed as his arm comes to rest on me again. I push it off.

"Ciara, when you are done playing your little game. I sure hope you end up alone. It's what you deserve after what you did to me. Grams' grand plan of finding you a husband is probably going to fail. No man wants to marry a slut. I am here on business, and they gave me tickets for the weekend, coincidence to run into you here."

I look up at Jasper and his eyes are pinned on me. I move away from Hunter again. I look for one of his bodyguards so that I can get the hell away from Hunter. When the song ends, I look over my shoulder and Jasper is kneeling down, talking to Victoria. She looks right at me, phew, she's going to get me out of here.

As Jasper and I headed to the bus, I could tell he was pissed. What I couldn't tell is if it was at me. I didn't do anything wrong. I went happily with Victoria to the side of the stage and stayed there with Cynthia until the concert ended. I didn't ask for Hunter to be near me. I didn't even know the asshole was in Ohio. So if Jasper is pissed at me, he is wrong.

It isn't until we are on the bus that he speaks to me. *"Do you know that guy?"*

"I do. I was dating him when Grams auctioned me off to you. His name is Hunter."

"I don't like his hands on you."

"I don't like it either. Come to think of it, I didn't like the hands of your fans all over your body, either. But we can't control the actions of other people."

"Ciara, I am sorry if I came across as being mad at you. I am not mad at you."

"Well, good because you have no reason to be. I didn't do anything wrong."

"That guy was the man staring at you at the store back home. He's following you."

"Are you sure? He told me he was in Ohio on business and tickets to the weekend were a bonus."

"I don't believe him. You shouldn't either. How convenient he was in Tennessee and now Ohio."

"I don't keep tabs on Hunter."

"It seems he is keeping tabs on you."

"I think you are overreacting."

"Am I? Are you sure he isn't the asshole who destroyed your shop? I saw the way he was looking

at you. He's jealous enough to want revenge for your breakup."

"I don't know, Jasper. I can have the cops look into it, but I think you are wrong."

"If it's not him, we have to find out who it is. I don't want you to leave me without knowing. I won't feel comfortable about sending you off and not knowing if the woman I care about is safe or not."

"I'm going to call Grams."

"I'm going to tell my driver we are ready and give you some privacy."

I waited until Jasper got off the bus to call Grams. I feel Jasper is wrong on this one, but I could be wrong. I just don't see why Hunter would go after my shop. It's not like he wanted to be around me much when we were together. He didn't seem all that into me when we were together so why would he destroy my shop, or better yet, why follow me to Tennessee and Ohio? It doesn't make sense to me.

CHAPTER THIRTEEN
CIARA

This month with Jasper has flown by. I am leaving for home at midnight tonight. This month had some challenges early on, but once we got back to the ranch after the jamboree everything went smoothly. We spent a lot of time really getting to know each other. I learned about Jasper as a person and not a country music star. He's really an amazing person, very in tune with who is and picks up on my feelings. Jasper has a way of knowing when something isn't right with me. When I was feeling down because we still have no idea if Hunter is my stalker or not, he reassured me we'll find out. If I showed any kind of worry at all for anything, he was on top of it making sure my mind was at ease. The two of us laughed a lot and I feel very comfortable at the ranch. It has really started to feel like I'm at home. I have grown to love his sense of humor and his cockiness.

Everything about Jasper that I have learned fits his personality to a T.

Once we got over the small humps in the beginning, our relationship really took on a whole new light. There is no denying our sexual relationship was hot from the start, but once we got settled back at the ranch, our sex life turned up the heat. I had a feeling Jasper was a dominant man from the start. We were back at the ranch for only a few days when I got to experience just how right I was. He took the time to tell me the lifestyle he likes to live and asked me if I would be okay with giving it a try. I knew from being with Kaiden what some of it entailed, but Jasper's was different in ways I didn't think I'd like. Jasper wanted me to give him complete control. By that I mean, he wanted more than just control in the bed and with the BDSM stuff. He wanted to set my schedule, tell me what I could and could not do. For instance, he would wake me every morning early to start my day with him. He picks my clothes when we go out in public and I'm absolutely not allowed to drink. There was more to it but that was the idea. If I did something Jasper didn't like, I had to allow him to punish me whatever way he saw fit. I didn't know if I could do it because I'm an independent person and not used to someone telling me what to do. I agreed to try it for a couple of days. When it was all said and done, I was not very good at having someone dictate my day. The punishments were fun, but I am who I am. I can't change everything about me and the way I live my life. Even though I care very deeply for him and he does me, it just didn't work. We found some even ground for the rest of our time together.

Now that we are at the end of our time together I'm going to have to decide if he might be the one for me. I am unsure if my feelings for him are as deep as they are for some of the other guys. It's just another hurdle I'm going to have to figure out later. I am worried that I didn't bend enough for his lifestyle. Jasper is used to doing things his way. I understand that about him because of his accomplishments. He didn't become who he is without discipline and being in control of himself. There is one thing I didn't quite understand about him, how did he decide his lifestyle? He said himself he hasn't had a relationship for many years. It's one thing I need to ask him before I leave tonight. I'm curious and want to understand his control issues fully. I probably should have asked weeks ago, but it is what it is.

I've been helping Cynthia cook up a storm today. She wanted to send me off with a little get together with everyone. Jasper thought it was a great idea. I'm a bit nervous as his mother Donita is coming over to meet me. Jasper says she's a very nice woman even though their relationship was rocky for a bit. I guess selling the ranch caused problems between them. Donita wanted nothing more to do with the ranch and was upset Jasper bought it. He said things got rough between them for over a year. Eventually, they made up and moved on. I guess Donita doesn't come around very much. It feels nice knowing she is coming over to meet me despite not wanting to be here.

"You know you should be spending time with Jasper instead of helping me. Everything is about all set here. You should go find that man of yours and be with him."

"Thanks, I'm going to do just that!"

I am out the door before she can change her mind. I see Jasper right away over by the gate that leads to the horse pasture. He has one foot up on the bottom railing and his left arm is slumped over the top one. Anyone who didn't know him would think he's just watching the horses, but I know him pretty well. Jasper is deep in thought. I know this because he had his first two fingers against his lips. When he does that, he's thinking.

"Whatcha thinking about, Mr. Collins?"

His head tilts so that he can see me over his shoulder. His foot goes to the ground and his arm falls from the railing. He doesn't say a word. Instead, he grabs me by the hand and takes off toward the inside of the barn. I laugh as I just about trip over my own two feet. When we get inside, he takes me to the office he has set up. I raise my brow when he locks the door. He is very quick when he lifts me off my feet and sets me down on top of the desk.

"I'm thinking about how much I'm going to miss this." He leans in and kisses me. I spread my legs as his body moved in closer. His hands hold my face as his lips leave mine. *"I don't want to let you go. I know that I have to, but I don't like it. It's going to drive me crazy knowing I have no control over the outcome of our relationship."*

"Did I give you enough?"

"You have given me everything that I want in a relationship. One month isn't enough time with you."

"I agree."

"Have I given you enough to want to be with me when this is over?"

"You have given me enough of you to know that there's a very good possibility of that happening. A couple of weeks ago I told you I would be honest with you. That hasn't changed. I do have strong feelings

for you and I can see a wonderful future between us. However, I do have a strong connection with some of the other guys, as well. It's too hard to know right now. I have to sort out all these emotions and connections."

"I understand that I guess. It's going to be rough waiting to know your final decision. My bed is going to be cold without you in it."

Jasper steps back away from me. *"Are you alright?"*

"I have to know something before you go today."
"Okay, what is it?"
"If you pick me, are you willing to give up your life in New York?"
"You mean completely?"
"I'm not going to pretend that I will move to New York because I won't. My home is here and I want you to be part of that. Can you see yourself living on my ranch?"
"You want me to give up my career?"
"Of course not! We can find you a place in town or wherever you want to set up a shop. I'm just being honest with you, I don't see myself living anywhere other than here. If you don't want to be here or can't see yourself here, then it might help make your choice easier."

I see the worry weighing on his shoulders that I won't move for him if he's the one. I love his ranch, I just don't know if I could do well here with my clothing line. If Jasper is the one, I know that I would have to move here. When I first saw him here, I knew that this is where his heart is. I also know that some of the other guys are willing to compromise. Some have told me they are willing to move for me or figure out a way to split our living arrangements. It's just another thing I have to figure out later.

"You've given me something to think about. I don't really like that you said it's you and the ranch or nothing."

"I know it sounds selfish and it's pretty much a dick move. I want an answer today, but I am not going to force you to give me one. I just need you to know this is who I am. If you want me, you get the ranch as well. I think we could make a beautiful life here. Fill the house with kids and grow old together."

"I can't fault you for being a hundred percent honest with me. I get it, it's the whole package deal or we can't work."

"There's one last thing I need you to know."
"Okay."

"I want you as much as I wanted to be a country music singer, as much as I wanted to keep this ranch

in my family. I have fallen in love with you. If you come here in November, I would marry you come December in a heartbeat."

"*Thanks for telling me that.*" Jasper stares into my eyes. I see he is telling me the truth. *"Come here."* He stands between my legs again and I run my fingers through his beard. *"I have fallen for you too. If that love outweighs the others, I will gladly move here with you."*

Jasper puts his forehead to mine. *"That's hope. I'll take that answer."* He then kisses me.

We hear knocking on the office barn door and Cynthia telling us the food is ready. Jasper groans. When I jump down from the desk, he tells me if I moan even once during eating, he's going to bring me back in here and use the rope and crop that is on the desk on me before I leave. I see dinner is going to light my taste buds on fire.

CHAPTER FOURTEEN
CIARA

As I sit in my seat on the plane in first class I am instantly reminded of Jasper. He was true to his word about if I moaned during eating. After dinner was all taken care of he took me out to the barn where he stripped me down to nothing. He bent me over his desk and bound my wrists then tied the rope to the feet of the desk. I couldn't move. My body was his for whatever punishment he wanted to give. His hands began to massage my shoulders, my back, then just when I was relaxed enough, the first smack of his palm spanked my ass. When I thought the sting was going to stop, he used the crop on me. He talked to me between each lashing, telling me how I failed to comply with his command. My body was loving everything he was giving me. I took my punishment and while I was still bent over his desk, I was rewarded with him giving me an orgasm. An orgasm I won't forget any time soon. Especially with my ass still on fire. Every move I make, my jeans remind me of what he did. Even though it stings, it is a welcomed reminder.

I sit back in my seat and put my earbuds in. I hit play on the mini recorder Jasper gave me. His voice comes to life in my ears. I close my eyes and listen.

"First thing you need to do is uncross your legs. Can you feel the touch of my fingers leaving a trail of goosebumps as my fingers travel up to your thigh? I can hear the gasps that you just made. Your hands are gripping the armrest as my finger grazes your clit through your panties. I'm hard as fuck just thinking about being inside you. Relax and let the moment take you away." There is a long pause. *"You should be in the air by now just like the first time we met, but don't open your eyes yet. I wrote you a song."*

I don't open my eyes as he said. I got more lost in his voice. He sings a song about falling in love with a girl that stole his heart. Tears leak from under my lids. This man has my heart doing pitter-patters. I think I fell a little deeper in love with him just now.

I listen to the song and when it ends he tells me he loves me. I whisper, I love you too. I want to jump out of my seat and demand to be taken back to Tennessee. I know it's not possible. Not yet anyway.

The rest of my flight I think about my time with Jasper. Not only did he welcome me into his life but his entire team did. The ranch crew felt like family. The bodyguards, the band, and his manager treated me like a friend. It is now that I see I would be gaining more than just a lover, a husband if I end up with Jasper - I'd be gaining an entire family. Grams is my family. Porter is my family. That is all I have. My family would grow bigger than I ever thought possible. Jasper would give me all that and more.

I exit the plane and Grams driver or bodyguard is waiting for me. I am looking forward to putting my arms around Grams. I can't wait to see Alaska. I wish that I had taken her with me. She would have loved all the room to roam the ranch.

I got into the backseat and turned my cell phone on. I get an alert as soon as it's powered on. I read the message. My heart sinks.

Malcolm: My home was burned. I'm alright. I wasn't at home at the time. I wanted to be the one to tell you before you heard it on the news. The fire was intentional.

So many questions instantly fill my thoughts. I try to call him, but it goes to voicemail. How does he know it was intentional? Is this my fault? Has my stalker moved on to the guys I'm dating? Someone needs to do their job and catch this asshole!

Me: I am home, please call me! I am so sorry this has happened to you. Please be careful.

I wipe my tears eyes as anger sets in. Whoever this person is needs to be stopped before they hurt someone or worse. I tell Grams' driver to hurry up and get me home. My heart rate picks up just thinking about the possibility that they may come after her. I cannot lose the only person who had ever been there for me.

ABOUT THE AUTHOR

Thank you so much for taking the time to read Grandma's Silent Auction - July. Word-of-mouth is crucial for any author to succeed. If you enjoyed the book, please leave a review on Amazon. Even if it's just a sentence or two. It would make all the difference and would be very much appreciated. – OXOX Michael James

Michael's Links:

Website: http://michaeljames-author332.bravesites.com/

ALSO BY MICHAEL JAMES

If you enjoyed Grandma's Silent Auction - July, you may also like my other books:

The Way We Love series:

Pink Skies At Night

Shadows At Night

Nights Are Unlimited

Concealed By The Night

Shattered At Night

Freed At Night

Winning A Cowgirl's Heart - Trilogy:

The Rodeo King

The Best Friend

The Fate Of My Heart

Winning a Cowgirl's Heart -Complete Box Set

Construction Vs. Corporate- Trilogy:

Unbalanced

Balancing

Balanced

Secrets Within a Club

Club Comrade

Revenge

Saving Club Conrad

Masquerade Saga

His Pearls

His Secrets

His Prison

His Games

His Moves

All His

Crime in Landkaster series

The Mirror

Times Like These

Lonely Road of Faith

Grandma's Silent Auction series

January

February

March

April

May

June

Lost Love Letter

I'll be Waiting

Before I Do

Standalone:

Toying With October

Pieces Of Me

A Christmas For Eve

Dom Diaries: Tangled Up In You

Christmas Scavenger Hunt

Blue Christmas

Stealing the Christmas Spotlight

Co-written with Jodi Fahey

Last Sheet

Co-written with Daniel Grayson

Inside the Storm

Made in United States
Cleveland, OH
06 April 2025

15838751R00059